characters created by lauren child

I am EXTREMELY absolutely boiling

PUFFIN

Text based on the script written by Bridget Hurst

Illustrations from the TV animation produced by Tiger Aspect

PUFFIN BOOKS
Published by the Penguin Group: London, New York, Australia,
Canada, India, Ireland, New Zealand and South Africa
Penguin Books Ltd, Registered Offices: 80 Strand, London WC2R 0RL, England

puffinbooks.com

This edition published in Great Britain in Puffin Books 2010
1 3 5 7 9 8 6 4 2

Manufactured in China
ISBN: 978-0-141-33495-0
This edition produced for The Book People Ltd,
Hall Wood Avenue, Haydock, St Helens, WA11 9UL

I have this little sister Lola.
              She is small and very funny.
"I am also extremely absolutely BOILING!
        And the only thing that will make me completely
NOT boiling any more is a strawberry ice cream!"

Outside in the shade,
I ask, "Arnold, why are
you panting?"

Arnold says,
"Dogs keep cool by panting.
I'm trying to see
if it works."

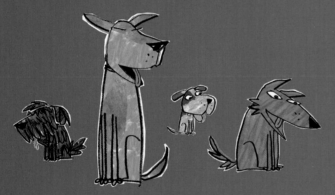

Lola says,
"Could you pant
more quieter please?"

Then I say,
"I hear the ice-cream truck!"

Lola says,
        "Yum, strawberry!"

"Mmm... yummy,"
        says Arnold.

Then Lola says,
        "I know, Arnold!
I'll taste your ice cream
and then you can
                taste mine."

"OK. Me first,"
        says Arnold.

Arnold takes a big lick
of Lola's ice cream,
        but when Lola
tries to take it back...

"Oh no!" shouts Lola.
"My ice cream is COMPLETELY
all over the floor!"

"Maybe Arnold
will **share** his ice cream
with you," I say.

So Lola asks,
"Arnold, will you share your
ice cream with me?"

But Arnold says, "No."

And Lola says,
"You are not my
favourite or my **best**.
I will not ever
never forgive you!"

Later, Lola says,
"Ice is good
for **cooling**, but not
as nice-tasting
as ice cream."

"I wish we were in
the North Pole," I say.

"Yes," Lola says.
"Where it is completely
freezing cold."

Marv and Morton pass by
on their way to
the swimming pool.

Lola asks,
"Can we come, too?"

But Marv says,
"Sorry, Lola. There isn't any
room in the car.
Maybe you could
play with Arnold?"

"I'm not playing
with him," says Lola.
"He's a MeaNie!"

Instead of going
to the pool,
    Lola and I make
a waterfall.

"All the water's gone,"
    Lola says.

"That's OK," I say.
    "We'll get more
from the hose."

That's when we see
Arnold... and his pool.

So I say,
"That would DEFINITELY
        cool us down.
Don't you think,
                Lola?"

But Lola says,
"Come on, Charlie..."

"It might be a really,
       really good idea to
forgive Arnold," I say.
              "Then maybe you
can play in a real pool."

"But he didn't share
              OR say he's sorry,"
says Lola.

"Well, he looks sorry," I say.

"Does he?" Lola asks.

       Then Arnold calls out,
"Lola, would you like
              to sit in my pool?"

Lola finally says,
"Yes, please."

And Arnold says,
"I'm sorry about the ice cream, Lola."

"That's OK," says Lola.
"Do you want to play squirty bottles?"

"Yes, please," he says.

"Charlie!" Lola shouts.
"Can you pass Arnold a squirty bottle?"

"I can't," I say. "Arnold's dad gave us ice lollies!"

"ICE LOLLIES!" Lola says.

PLOP!
Arnold's ice lolly falls
                into the pool.

"My ice lolly!" says Arnold.

So Lola asks,
"Do you want a bit of mine?"

And Arnold says,
        "Thanks, Lola."

But then...

PLOP!
Lola's ice lolly falls into the pool, too.
"Oops," Arnold says.
And Lola says, "Charlie...?"